ADVENTURE TIME™

PIXEL PRINCESSES

ALSO AVAILABLE

Adventure Time Vol 1

Adventure Time Vol 2

Adventure Time Vol 3

Adventure Time:
Vol 1 Mathematical Edition

Adventure Time:
Vol 2 Mathematical Edition

Adventure Time:
Sugary Shorts

Adventure Time:
Marceline & The Scream Queens

Adventure Time:
Fiona & Cake

Adventure Time:
Playing with Fire

ADVENTURE TIME: PIXEL PRINCESSES. Published by Titan Comics, a division of Titan Publishing Group Ltd., 144 Southwark St., London, SE1 0UP. ADVENTURE TIME, CARTOON NETWORK, the logos, and all related characters and elements are trademarks of and © Cartoon Network. (S13) All rights reserved. All characters, events and institutions depicted herein are fictional. Any similarity between any of the names, characters, persons, events and/or institutions in this publication to actual names, characters, and persons, whether living or dead and/or institutions are unintended and purely coincidental.

A CIP catalogue record for this title is available from the British Library.

Printed in Spain.

First published in the USA and Canada in November 2013 by Kaboom!, an imprint of BOOM! Studios.

10 9 8 7 6 5 4 3 2 1

ISBN: 9781782760504

  www.titan-comics.com

Created by **PENDLETON WARD**
Written by **DANIELLE CORSETTO**
Illustrated by **ZACK STERLING**
With **TESSA STONE**
COREY LEWIS
CHRYSTIN GARLAND
PAULINA GANUCHEAU

Inks by **STEPHANIE HOCUTT**
and **AUBREY AIESE**
Tones by **AMANDA LAFRENAIS**
Letters by **KEL McDONALD**

"The Mind of Gunter" by **MEREDITH McCLAREN**
Tones by **AMANDA LAFRENAIS**

Cover by **STEPHANIE GONZAGA**

Assistant Editor **WHITNEY LEOPARD**
Editor **SHANNON WATTERS**
Designer **HANNAH NANCE PARTLOW**

With Special Thanks to Marisa Marionakis, Rick Blanco, Curtis Lelash, Laurie Halal-Ono,

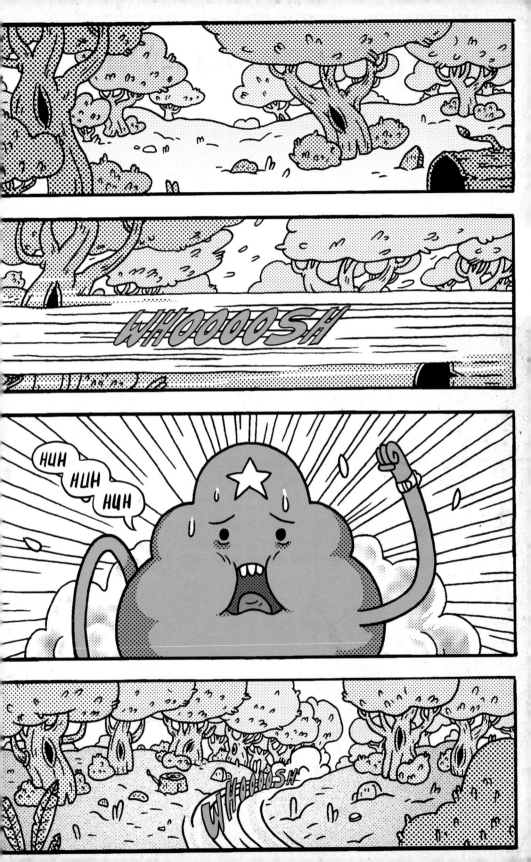

AND I BET *NONE* OF YOU EVEN *WANTS* TO BE HERE!

C'MON FESS UP!

WHY DID YOU COME TO MY PARTY?

BREAKFAST PRINCESS?

MY SIS AND I DREW STRAWS, AND I PULLED THE SHORT ONE.

I NEED ONE OF THOSE!

LSP, NO! YOU'RE GONNA GET *HURT!*

DO YOU EVEN UNDERSTAND?

I'M FLIPPIN' HOMELESS!

BONK

OW!

HEY!!

PLUCK

THAT WAS GONNA BE MY DOORKNOB!!

YOU DON'T *HAVE* A *DOOR!*

WHO THROWS A DOOR??

OUI OUI

EET EES *ME!*

I WEEL THROW THEE DOOR, AND THEE *WHOLE* HOUSE, TOO!

HYAH!

Congratulations!
You saved the princess!

HUH?

BMO? WHAT'S GOING ON?

OH, YOU ARE INSIDE OF ME!

BUT... HOW?

I WISHED ON A SHOOTING STAR!

YOU... WISHED FOR US TO BE INSIDE OF YOU?

YES.

THAT'S NORMAL.

NOPE.

BMO, DID YOU *EAT* US??

YUP.

GOODBYE!

READY?
5
SUIT UP!

ZOOP

BANG

THIS IS THE OPPOSITE OF SAFETY.

READY?

GO

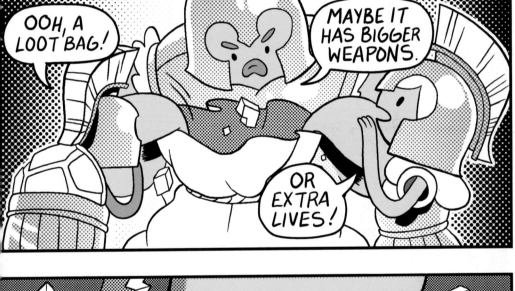

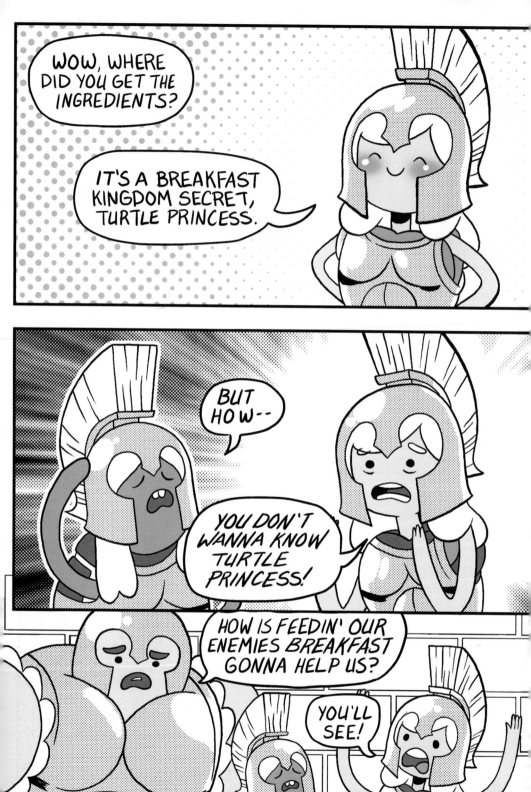

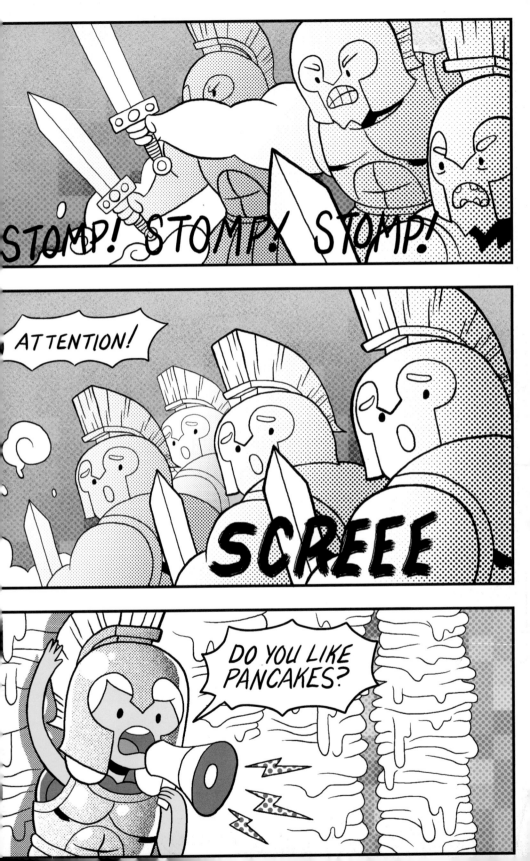

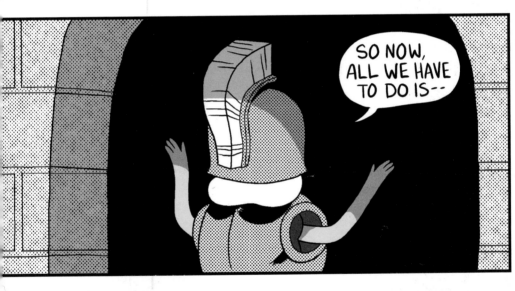

Congratulations!
You've saved the princess!

PRINCESS?

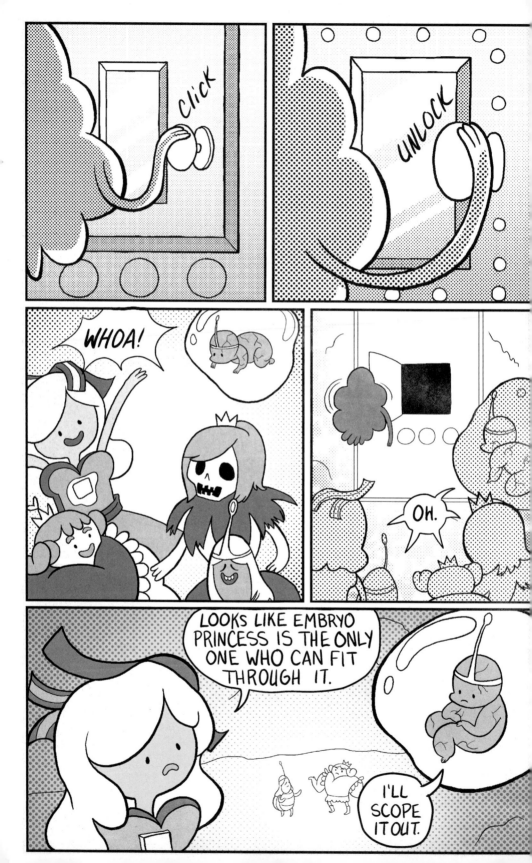

498 jumps later_

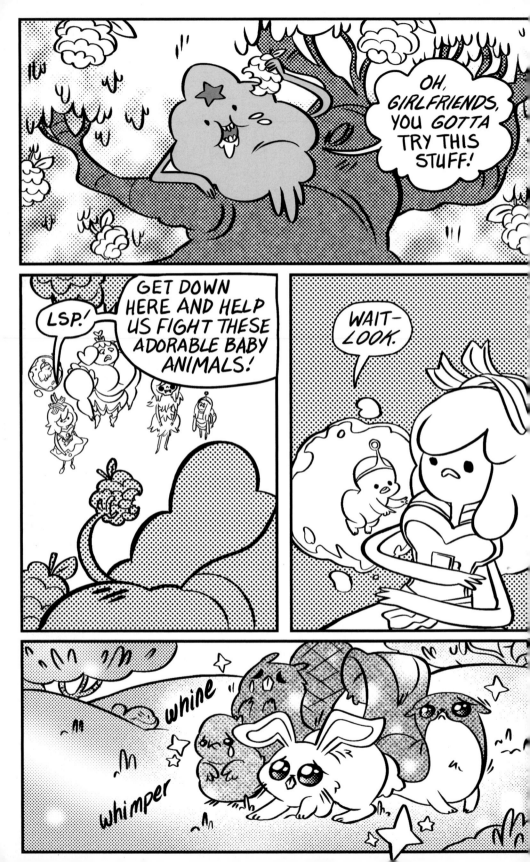

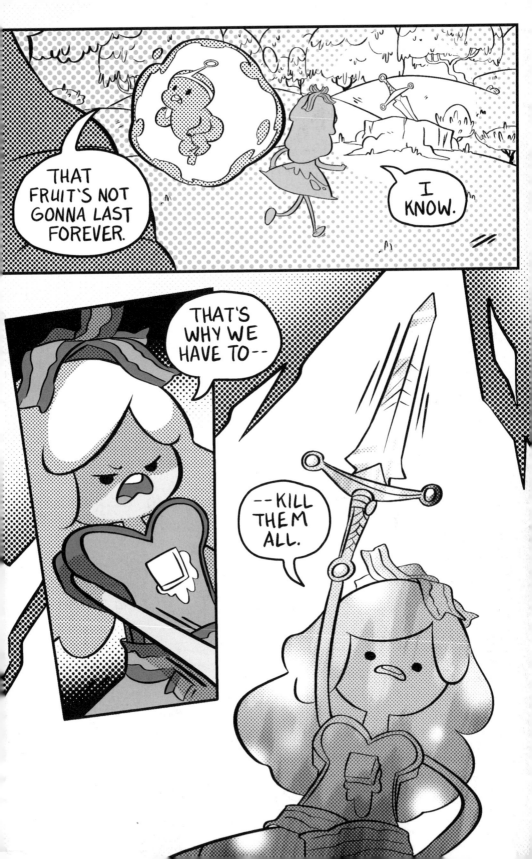

Congratulations!
You've saved the princess!

MEH.

AW, C'MON GUYS.

GET READY, TP--

--LOOKS LIKE SOMEONE HIT THE START BUTTON!

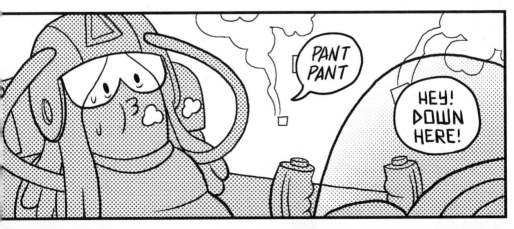

GOOD JOB, DANGER TURTLE, YOU GOT THEM ALL.

I DID?

YOU'RE MOMMY'S FAVORITE.

YOU GET DESSERT!

I DO?

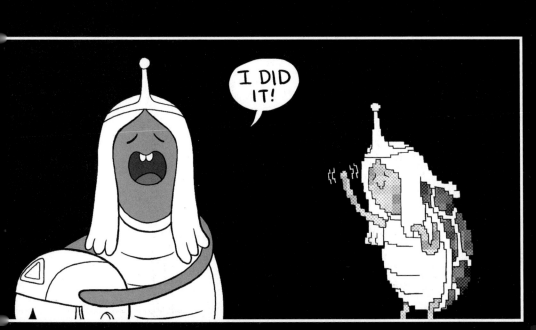

Congratulations! You've saved the princess!

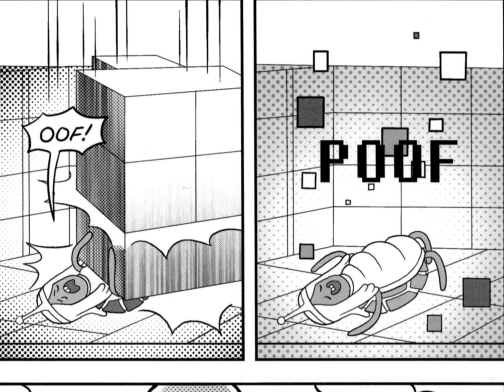

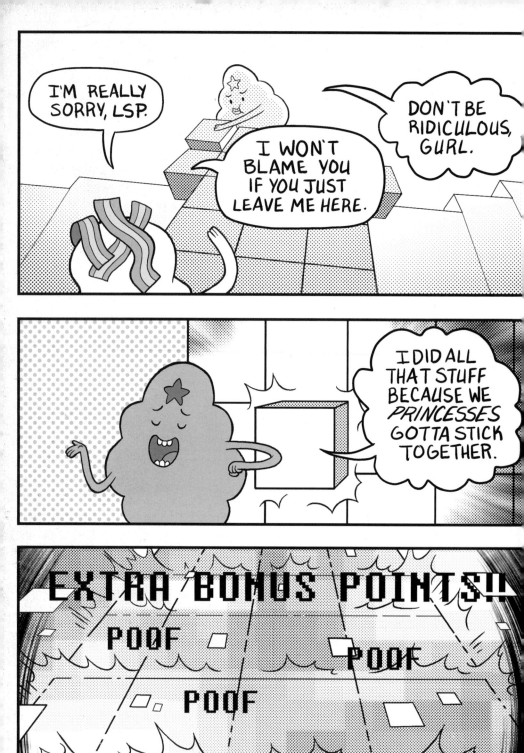

Congratulations!
You've saved the princesses!

HOORAY!

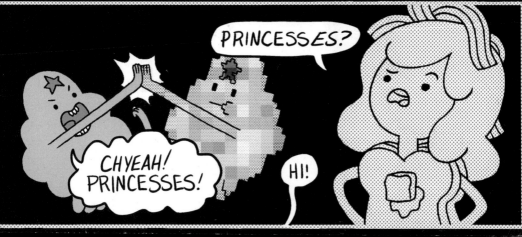

PRINCESSES?

CHYEAH! PRINCESSES!

HI!

EJECT

ZOOP

SURPRISE!

SORRY WE'RE LATE!

EVERYONE GOT READY AT MY PLACE, AND I ONLY HAVE LIKE ONE BATHROOM.

I FOUND THIS ON THE GROUND OUTSIDE. ISN'T IT YOURS, LSP?

MY GEM!

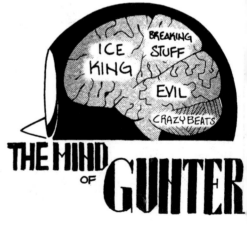

THE MIND OF GUNTER

THE END